For Elizabeth

Library of Congress Cataloging in Publciation Data
Barklem, Jill. The secret staircase. Brambly Hedge
Summary: Quite by accident, the young mice, Primrose
and Wilfred, find a secret staircase in the Old Oak
Palace which leads them to a magnificent surprise.
[1. Mice—fiction] I. Title. II. Series; Barklem,
Jill. Brambly Hedge
PZ7.B25058Se   1983   E   83–6270
ISBN 0-399-20994-8
ISBN (mini edition) 0-399-21865-3
First Miniature Edition
First American Edition published in 1983 by Philomel Books,
a division of The Putnam & Grosset Book Group,
200 Madison Avenue, New York, NY 10016.
Originally published in Great Britain by
Wm. Collins Sons & Co. Ltd.
Printed in Great Britain by
HarperCollins Manufacturing, Glasgow

THE SECRET STAIRCASE

Jill Barklem

PHILOMEL BOOKS
New York

It was a frosty morning. The air was crisp and cold and everything sparkled in the winter sunshine. The little mice hurrying along the path turned up their collars and blew on their paws in an effort to keep warm.

"Merry Midwinter," panted Dusty Dogwood, scurrying past Mr Apple and the

Toadflax children with a huge covered basket.
Mr Apple and the children were busy too,
dragging great sprays of holly and trails of ivy
and mistletoe towards the Old Oak Palace.
When they arrived at the gates, they heaped all
the branches on the ground and Wilfred tugged
on the bell.

Lord Woodmouse and Primrose, his daughter, opened the door.

"Here we are," said Mr Apple, mopping his face, "do you want it all inside?"

"Yes, please," said Lord Woodmouse. "We'll start by decorating the stairs." Eagerly, the children pulled the branches over the polished palace floors and skidded their way into the Great Hall.

"Are you two ready for tonight?" asked Lord Woodmouse.

Primrose and Wilfred exchanged glances. That evening, after dark, all the mice would gather round a blazing fire for the traditional midwinter celebrations. A grand entertainment was planned and Primrose and Wilfred had chosen to give a recitation.

"Almost," said Primrose, "but we've still got to practise and we need proper costumes."

"You'd better see your mother about those," replied her father. "You can practise wherever you like."

Leaving Clover, Catkin and Teasel to go back
to the wood with Mr Apple, Primrose and
Wilfred took themselves off to a corner of the
hall and began to go through their lines.

"When the days are the shortest, the nights are the coldest..."
began Primrose, drawing an imaginary cloak
around her.

"The frost is the sharpest, the year is the oldest..."
continued Wilfred.

"Look out, you two," interrupted Basil,
bustling past with some bottles.

"This is hopeless," sighed Primrose. "We can't
rehearse here. Let's go and ask Mama what to do."

Lady Woodmouse was busy making caraway biscuits in the kitchen. She leaned on her rolling pin to listen to Primrose's tale of woe.

"Why don't you see if there's something up in the attics for you to wear," she said. "You could practise up there too." She packed a little basket with bread and cheese and a jug of blackberry juice and shooed the children gently out of the kitchen.

There were a great many attic rooms at the top of Old Oak Palace. Lady Woodmouse used them to tidy away things that might come in useful. Babies' blankets and rolls of lace, boxes of buttons, stacks of books, broken toys, patchwork quilts, pudding cloths and old saucepans were all crammed together, higgledy-piggledy, on the shelves.

Primrose and Wilfred went from room to room looking for a suitable spot for their rehearsal. They ended up in a crowded storeroom at the end of a passage, but it was difficult to concentrate on practising, there were so many things to look at.

Standing on tiptoe, Primrose reached inside the drawer of an old wooden dresser. In it, she found some bundles of letters tied up in pink ribbon but she couldn't read the writing and as it's rude to read other people's letters, she put them back. As she did so, she caught sight of a small key which had slipped down at the side of the drawer.

"Look at this, Wilfred," she cried excitedly.

"Let's see. Oh, it's only an old key," said Wilfred. "Is it time for lunch?"

Primrose said nothing, but she slipped the key into her pinafore pocket before setting out their picnic on the floor.

"Do you think this would make a cloak?" said Wilfred, his mouth full of bread and cheese. He had seized the end of a long green curtain and was winding himself up in it. As he turned towards Primrose, he caught sight of a small door hidden behind its folds.

"Where does this go to, Primrose?" he asked.

"I don't know," replied Primrose, scrambling over some boxes. "Does it open?"

Wilfred pushed. The door was locked. He peeped through the keyhole and saw another flight of stairs on the other side of the door.

"It's no good," he said, disappointedly, "we can't get in."

"If there's a keyhole, there must be a key," said Primrose, "and I think I have it here!" She reached inside her pinafore pocket and handed the little key to Wilfred. He tried it in the lock. It fitted perfectly and the door swung open.

They found themselves in a dark panelled hall at the foot of a long winding staircase. The stair carpet must once have been beautiful, but now it was tattered and covered with dust.

"No one can have been up here for years and years," whispered Primrose. "Shall we see what's at the top?"

Wilfred nodded, so up the stairs they went, round and round. Primrose kept close behind Wilfred, she couldn't help feeling a little nervous. Suddenly the stairs came to an abrupt end. They were standing in yet another hall, and there ahead was yet another door, but this time it was huge and richly carved. They went up to it and Wilfred gave it a push. As the door opened, the children stared about them in amazement.

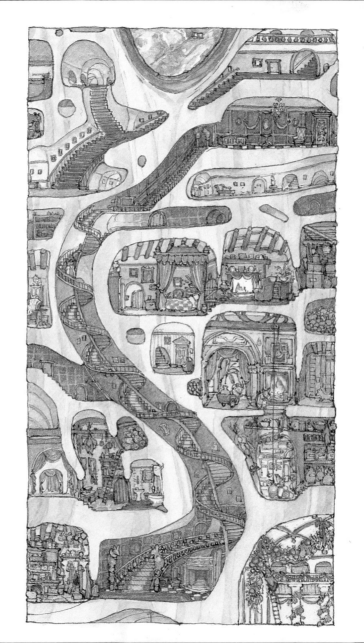

They were standing in the most magnificent room. There were columns and carvings, and dark tapestries and paintings on the walls. In front of them two golden chairs stood on a little platform. Everything in the room was covered in dust and the air smelled musty and strange.

"Where are we?" asked Wilfred.

"I don't know," whispered Primrose. "I've never been here before."

They tiptoed across the floor, leaving footprints as they went.

"Maybe your ancestors lived here in the olden days, Primrose," said Wilfred, gazing at an imposing portrait.

"Let's clean it all up and have it as our house," said Primrose. "We could keep it secret and come up here to play."

As she spoke, she opened a cupboard and found it full of hats.

"Wilfred! Look at these. They're just right for tonight!"

A door at the end of the room led into a nursery. There was a canopied cot near the window, and all sorts of dust-covered toys were on the shelves.

Wilfred peered inside an ancient trunk and pulled out a little suit with a high jacket and tight braided trousers. It was almost the right size for him. Neatly folded beneath it were dresses and cloaks, waistcoats and shawls, some trimmed with gold and others studded with shining stones. The children held them up, one after another, and each chose an outfit for the evening and tried it on.

"Perfect! And now we must practise."

"Let's finish exploring first," said Wilfred.

They seemed to be in a whole suite of rooms. There was a dining room, a butler's pantry, a small kitchen and several other bedrooms. The bathroom was particularly grand with a tiled floor and high windows. Wilfred rubbed a mirror clean and made faces at himself whilst Primrose leaned over the side of the bath to try the taps. No water came out.

"When the days are the shortest, the nights are the coldest..." she recited. Her voice sounded loud and echoey. Wilfred joined in, and they went through their lines again and again until they were word-perfect.

Outside the red sun was sinking low in the frosty air, and the bathroom was filled with shadows.

"It's getting late," said Primrose. "If we don't hurry, we'll miss the log."

They picked up their clothes and scampered over the dusty floors to the door.

Down the stairs they ran, round and round,
down and down, till they found themselves
back in the storeroom. They locked the door

with the little key and replaced it in the drawer.
Then they crept along the corridors to Primrose's
room, taking care to keep out of sight.

Primrose opened her window. They could just hear the carolling of the mice as the midwinter log was pulled along the hedge. There was no time to change, so they threw on their cloaks to hide their costumes and ran to join the crowd at the palace gates.

Mr Apple and Dusty Dogwood headed the procession, lanterns held high.

"Roast the chestnuts, heat the wine,
Pass the cups along the line,
Gather round, the log burns bright,
It's warm as toast inside tonight,"

sang the mice as the log came into view.

Teasel, Clover and Catkin were perched on the huge branch and as it was dragged up to the palace gates, Primrose and Wilfred scrambled up behind.

The mice pulled the log carefully over the threshold and Basil threw some bramble wine onto the bark. "Merry Midwinter!" he called.

At last the log was here. The midwinter celebrations could begin.

A fire had been laid ready in the hearth of the Great Hall and the log was rolled onto it. Everyone was handed a cup of steaming punch. Old Mrs Eyebright was to light the fire, and she held up a burning taper.

"To Summer!" she announced and Mr Apple stooped to help her thrust the taper into the fire.

"To Summer!" echoed the mice.

The bright flames licked the mossy bark and soon the log was ablaze. The mice helped

themselves to supper which was spread on a
table near the fire and Basil refilled their cups.

"Why don't you take off your cloak, dear?"
said Lady Woodmouse. "It's very hot here
by the fire."

"Not just yet, Mama," said Primrose.
"I'm still a bit chilly."

When they had eaten
all they could, they
drew their chairs up
round the hearth and
the entertainment began.
Mr Apple made huge shadows
on the wall by standing in front of
the fire. He made the shape of a weasel
with a mean little eye, and a snake's head,
a fox, and with the aid of a curtain, a bat.
The little mice squealed and laughed.
Next, Basil played a jig on his fiddle
and Dusty did some conjuring tricks.
Then they tried to pass a crabapple
right round the circle, holding it
under their chins, and after that
Lord Woodmose told stirring
tales of old times. Primrose and
Wilfred nudged each other.

Everyone did a turn until at last Lord Woodmouse said, "And now Primrose, what have you got for us?"

The children jumped up and took their places in front of the fire. Drawing their cloaks closely round them, they began:

MIDWINTER
When the days are the shortest, the nights are the coldest,
The frost is the sharpest, the year is the oldest,
The sun is the weakest, the wind is the hardest,
The snow is the deepest, the skies are the darkest,
Then polish your whiskers and tidy your nest,
And dress in your richest and finest and best...

For winter has brought you the worst it can bring,
And now it will give you
The promise of SPRING!

Primrose and Wilfred threw off their cloaks
and donned their hats with a flourish. The

audience gasped to see the beautiful clothes which sparkled in the firelight, and then clapped and cheered louder than ever. The applause went on for so long that Lord Woodmouse had to ask them to do it all over again.

At last, Primrose and Wilfred went back to their seats.

"That was wonderful!" whispered Lady Woodmouse, hugging her. "*Wherever* did you find those beautiful clothes?"

Primrose glanced quickly at Wilfred. "In the attic," she mumbled, hoping that her mother would not ask any more awkward questions. Luckily, at that moment, Basil started to tell one last story and everyone settled down to listen.

Primrose and Wilfred gazed at the fire and thought of all the lovely games they would play in their house at the top of the secret staircase. Soon their heads began to nod and in no time at all, they were both fast asleep.